RUSTY THE SQUEAKY ROBOT

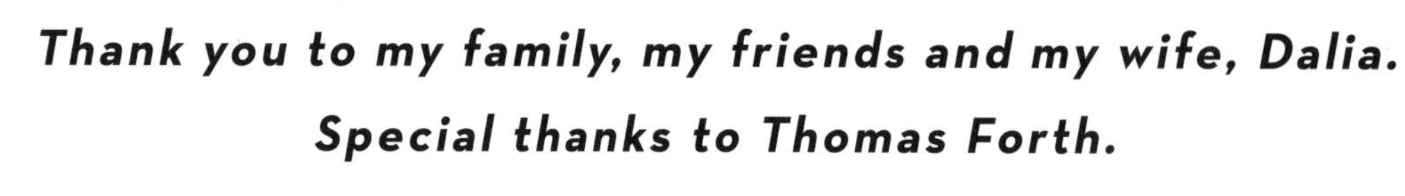

Thank you to my family, my friends and my wife, Dalia.

Special thanks to Thomas Forth.

Quarto is the authority on a wide range of topics.

Quarto educates, entertains and enriches the lives of our readers—enthusiasts and lovers of hands-on living.

www.quartoknows.com

This edition first published in 2018 by words & pictures,
an imprint of The Quarto Group.
26391 Crown Valley Parkway, Suite 220
Mission Viejo, CA 92691, USA
T: +1 949 380 7510
F: +1 949 380 7575
www.QuartoKnows.com

A CIP record for this book is available from the Library of Congress.

ISBN: 978-1-910277-52-2

Manufactured in Guangdong, China CC082020

9 8 7 6 5 4 3 2

MIX
Paper from responsible sources
FSC® C008047
FSC
www.fsc.org

RUSTY THE SQUEAKY ROBOT

by Neil Clark

words & pictures

Far, far away, on Planet Robotone,
Rusty the Robot felt sad and alone.

With every nod of his head
and tap of his feet,
he didn't much like
the way he went

He squeaked in the daytime

and squeaked through the night.

He squeaked so much it gave him a fright!

If he couldn't like his squeak, then he couldn't like himself.

If only on Planet Robotone there were robots who could help...

DING! Belle wheeled over,
she was cheery and bright.

“Don’t worry, Rusty,
I’ll make it all right.”

"There's no need to be sad,
all you need is a friend.
Let's go, follow me!
Let's see what's around the bend."

So off they went with
a **DING** and a **SQUEAK.**
I wonder who else Rusty
might meet?

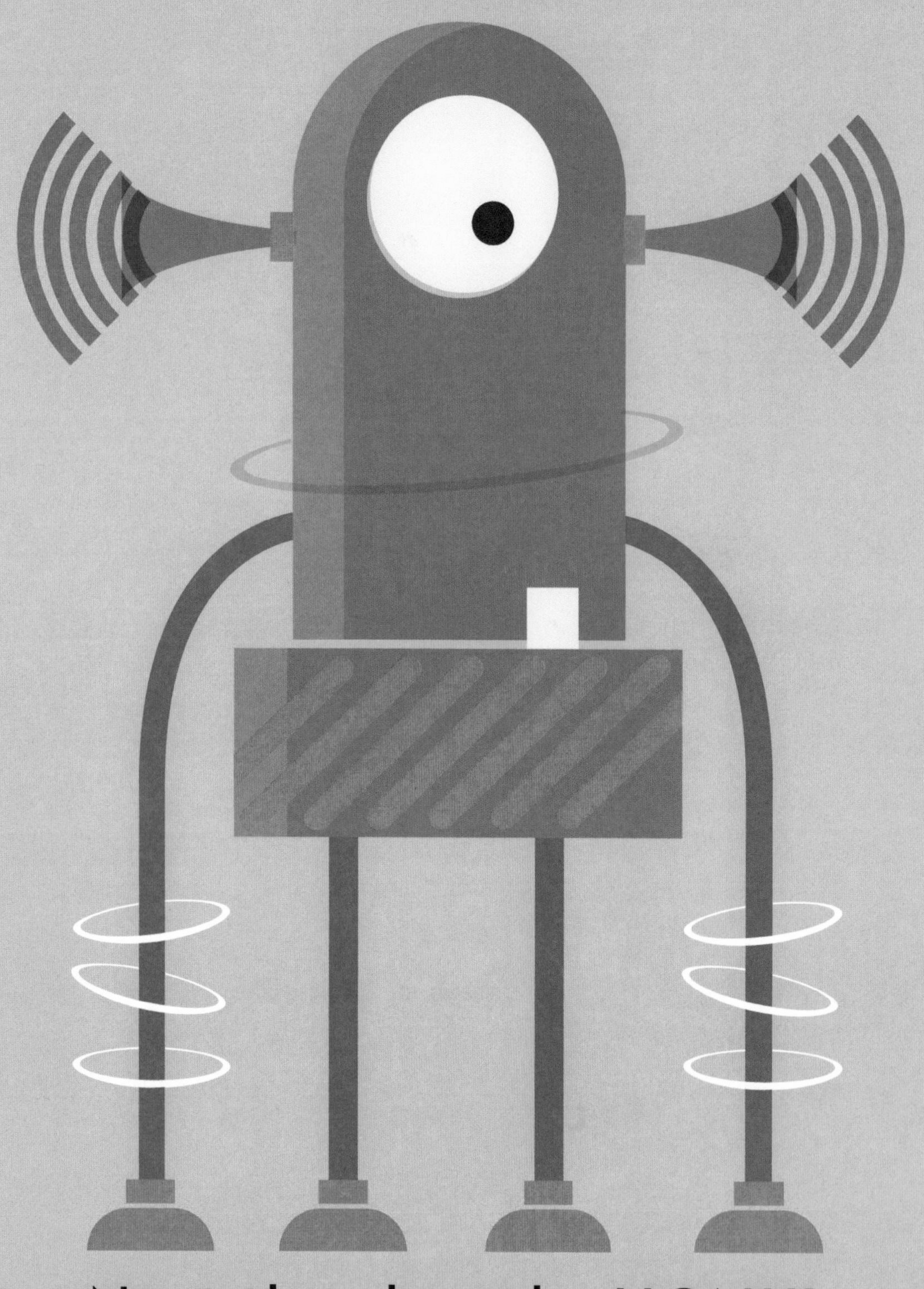

Next they heard a HONK!
Hoot had fun with his sound.

"Don't worry, Rusty,
there's no need
to feel down."

"Let's all loosen up, have fun, and play.
Enjoy yourself, Rusty, it's a much better way!"

So off they all went with
a **HONK, DING,** and **SQUEAK.**
Let's see who else
Rusty will meet.

A TWANG announced Twango.

He was so very smart.

"Don't worry, Rusty,
there's no need to
lose heart."

"We all have funny sounds,
but if we add them together...

...we can make brand *new* sounds,
it's really rather clever!"

So off they all went with a **TWANG, HONK, DING,** and **SQUEAK**. Rusty couldn't wait to see who else he would meet!

But a **BOOM** interrupted!
The noise shook the ground...

Look here, it's Boom-Bot!

He likes to play loud!

BOOM!
BOOM!
BOOM!

Boom-Bot said "Yo!" and pumped out a beat.
So the robots all moved and tapped their feet.

Rusty said: “I’m no longer worried about a thing!”

“It’s OK to be different. It’s OK to be me.”

"My sound makes me special.

That's how we should all be."

And so with a nod, tap, skip, and leap,

Rusty said: "Now I love the way I go...